GORAM & GHYSTON
THE BRISTOL GIANTS

For Wilf and Gilby – thank you for inspiring me to write this book.

Goram & Ghyston THE BRISTOL GIANTS

BY OLIVER RIGBY

ILLUSTRATED BY TOM BONSON

Some people say that Giants are scary. Some people say that Giants don't exist.
Clearly, those people have never met a Giant before!

Giants are brilliant. They are kind and clever and very strong. With their massive arms,
they have made rivers, lakes and mountains and they even threw the moon into the sky.

Most Giants live in a beautiful city called Bristol. They are very good at hiding but if you look
carefully you may just spot one.

This story is about the first Bristol Giants and how they came to form the landscape of the city as it now stands. It is a very, very old story that has nearly been forgotten, so listen well.

Once upon a time, many years ago, there were two brothers called Goram and Ghyston. They were no ordinary brothers – they were GIANTS.

Goram and Ghyston were the largest of all the Giants and they lived by a Great Lake that covered the lands where Bristol now stands.

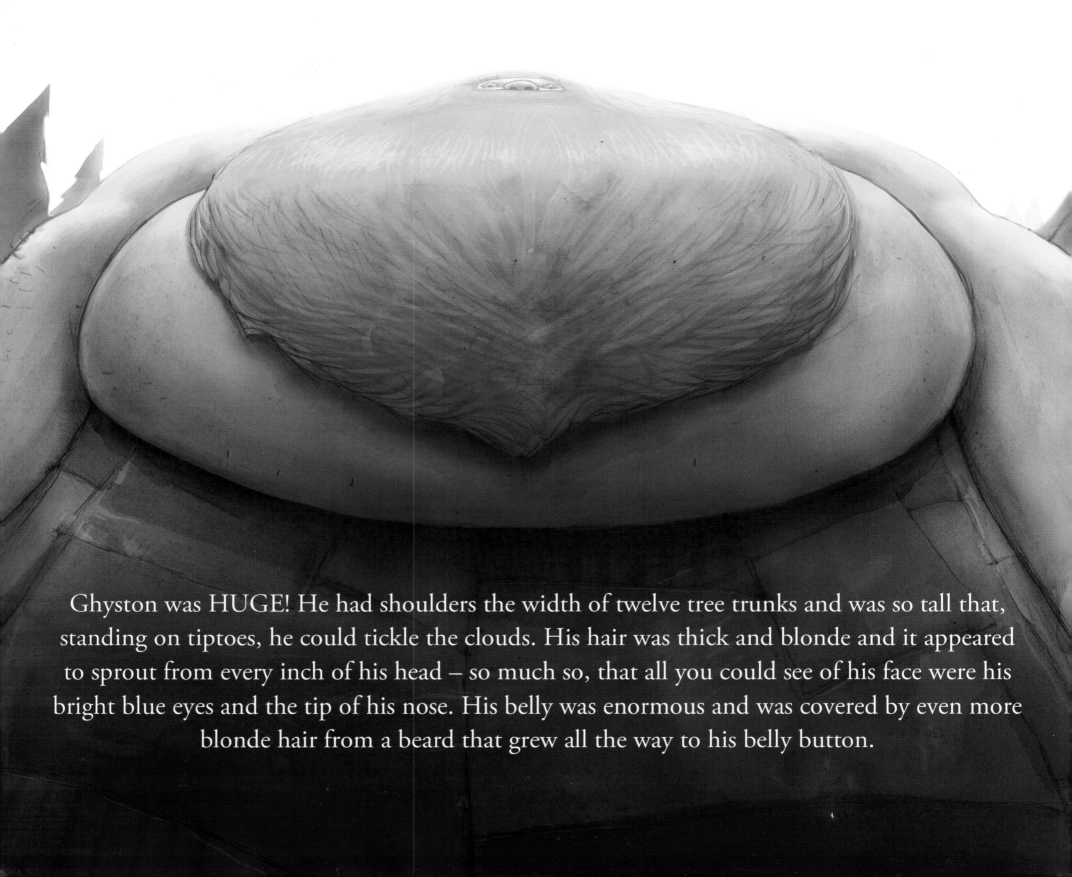

Ghyston was HUGE! He had shoulders the width of twelve tree trunks and was so tall that, standing on tiptoes, he could tickle the clouds. His hair was thick and blonde and it appeared to sprout from every inch of his head – so much so, that all you could see of his face were his bright blue eyes and the tip of his nose. His belly was enormous and was covered by even more blonde hair from a beard that grew all the way to his belly button.

Goram was even taller than Ghyston, but skinnier
(if you can call a Giant skinny) and with feet the size of
fishing boats. His eyes were bright blue like his brother's but
he was almost completely bald. All his hair had been burnt off
by his pet dragon, Digby, after a nasty case of dragon flu resulted in
an explosion of fiery bogeys!

The Brothers lived happily together chasing dinosaurs and surfing with whales, until one day they happened upon Princess Avona.

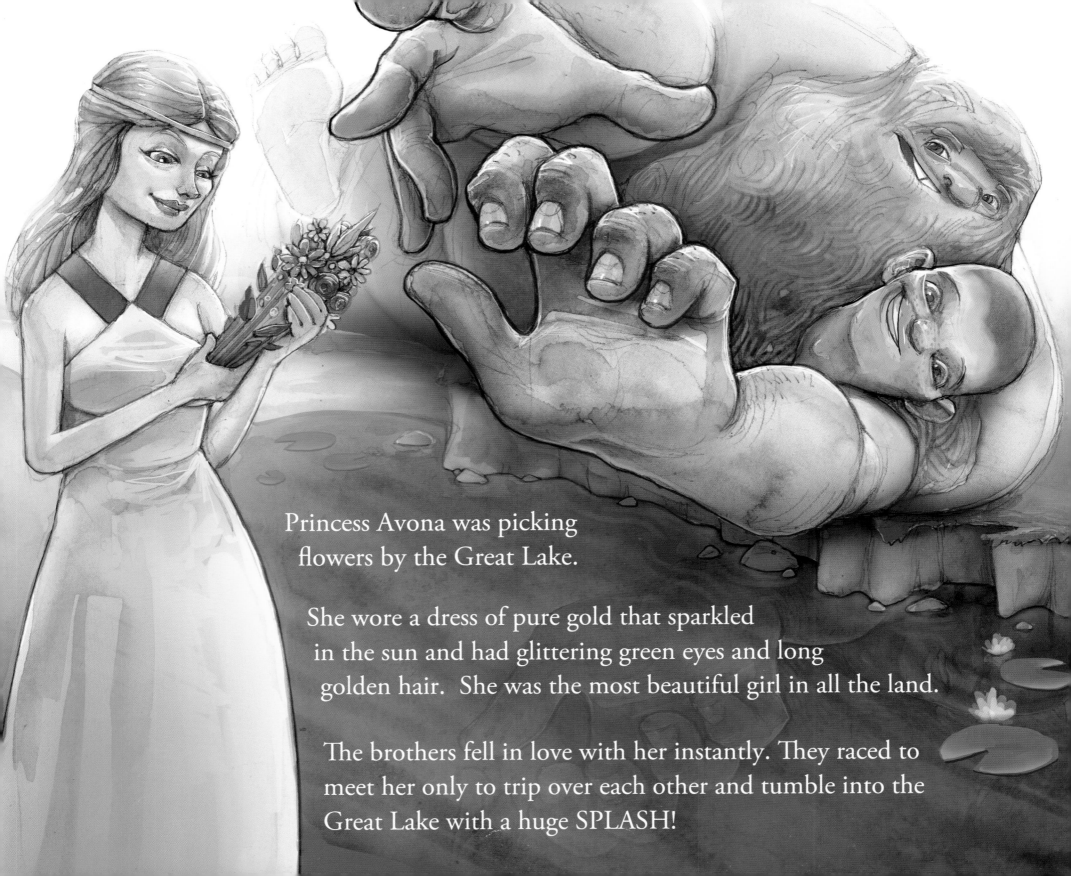

Princess Avona was picking
flowers by the Great Lake.

She wore a dress of pure gold that sparkled
in the sun and had glittering green eyes and long
golden hair. She was the most beautiful girl in all the land.

The brothers fell in love with her instantly. They raced to
meet her only to trip over each other and tumble into the
Great Lake with a huge SPLASH!

Princess Avona laughed at the wet muddle of arms and legs splashing and crashing in the water.

"Hello," said a Giant, snatching breaths from between his brother's legs, "I am Goram."

"And I am Ghyston," spluttered the other as he tried to remove one of Goram's toes from his nostril.

The Giants were overcome with love and tried desperately to impress Princess Avona.

"Can I catch you a dinosaur?" yelled Goram.
"Can I catch you a whale?" bellowed Ghyston.
"I love you!" they both swooned together. This was
followed by thumps and calls of "I saw her first," and
"Gerr off, she's mine," as the bickering brothers
disappeared back under the water in a burst of bubbles.

Princess Avona giggled. "What a sight – two Giants in love with me!
What on earth shall I do?"

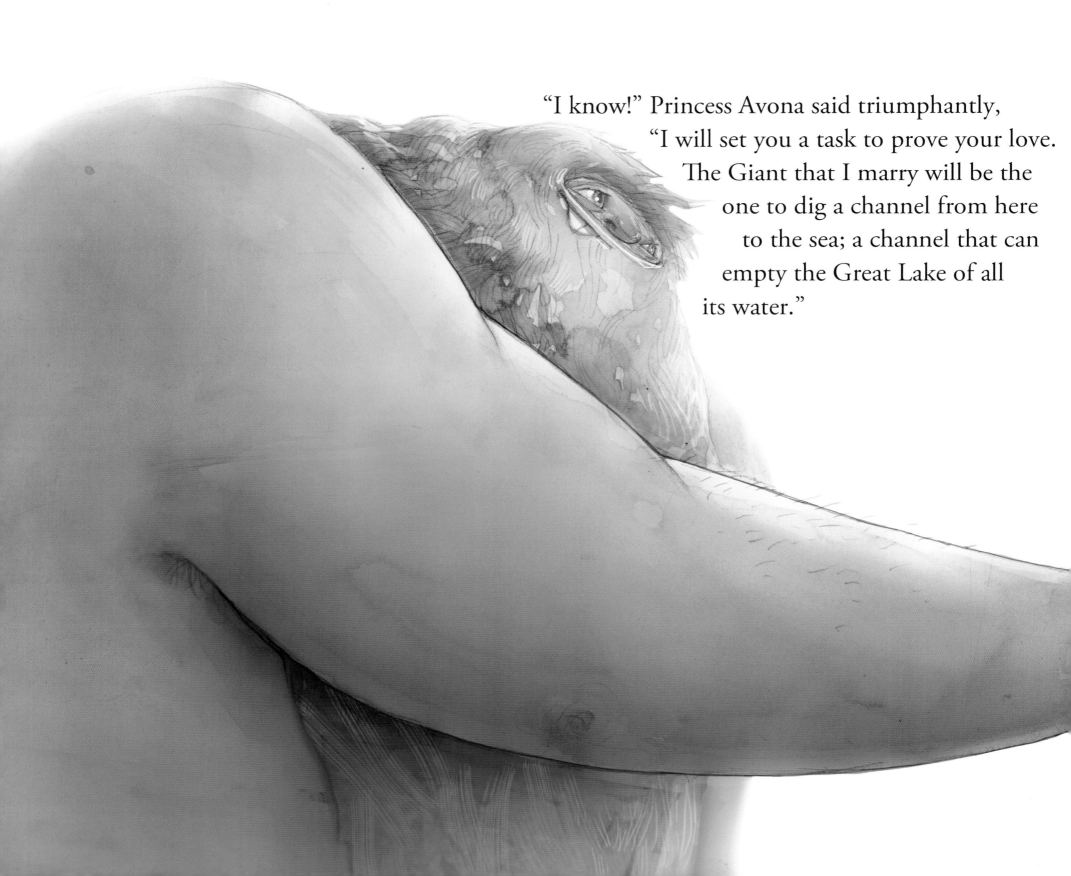

"I know!" Princess Avona said triumphantly,
"I will set you a task to prove your love.
The Giant that I marry will be the
one to dig a channel from here
to the sea; a channel that can
empty the Great Lake of all
its water."

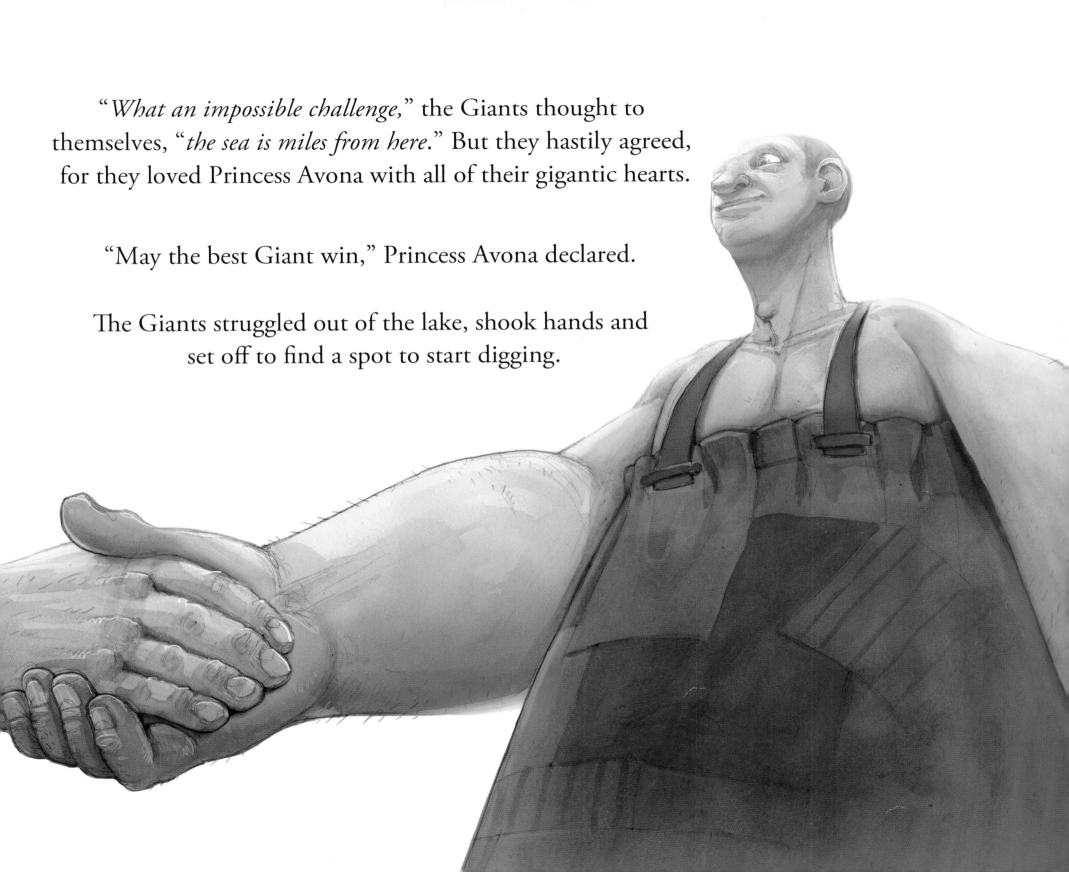

"*What an impossible challenge,*" the Giants thought to themselves, "*the sea is miles from here.*" But they hastily agreed, for they loved Princess Avona with all of their gigantic hearts.

"May the best Giant win," Princess Avona declared.

The Giants struggled out of the lake, shook hands and set off to find a spot to start digging.

It was a very long way to the sea and the task would take them many weeks.
Goram and Ghyston started digging and as they dug they sang.

"Princess Avona has set us a task, to empty this lake to the sea,
We'll dig and we'll dig until it's all done, and the Princess is married to ME."

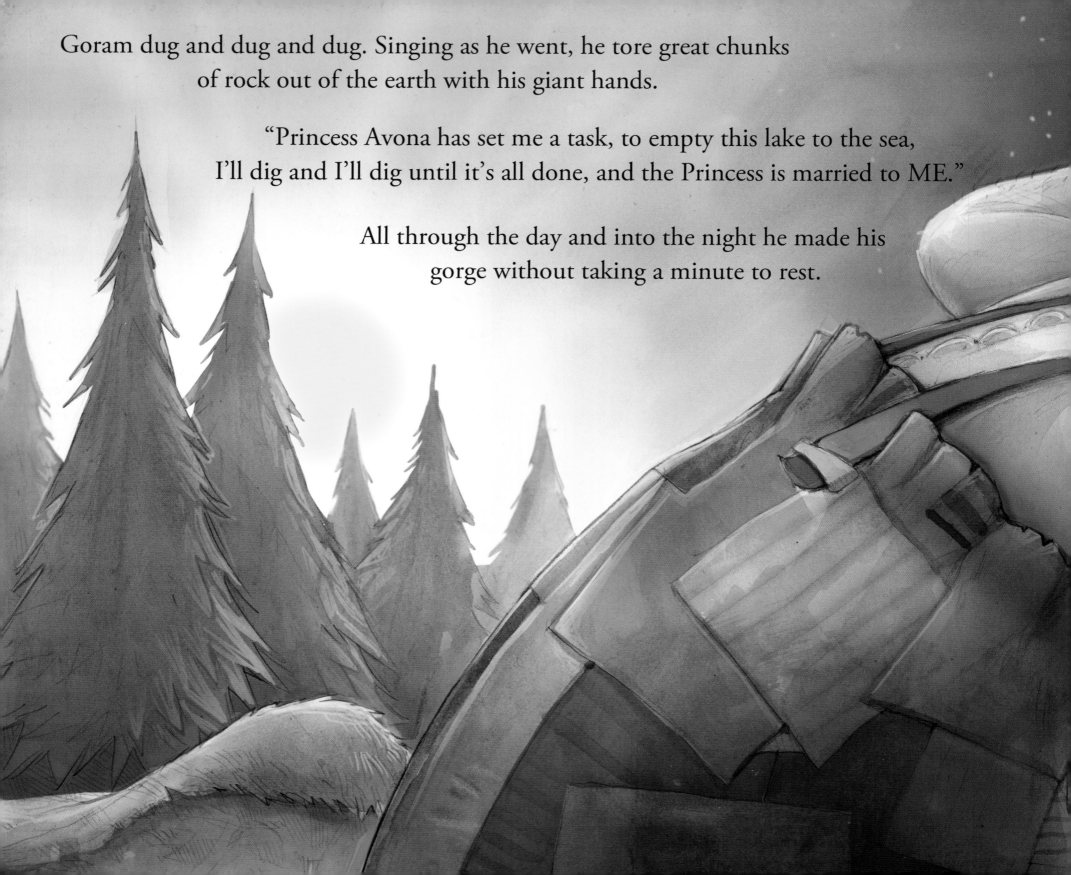

Goram dug and dug and dug. Singing as he went, he tore great chunks
of rock out of the earth with his giant hands.

"Princess Avona has set me a task, to empty this lake to the sea,
I'll dig and I'll dig until it's all done, and the Princess is married to ME."

All through the day and into the night he made his
gorge without taking a minute to rest.

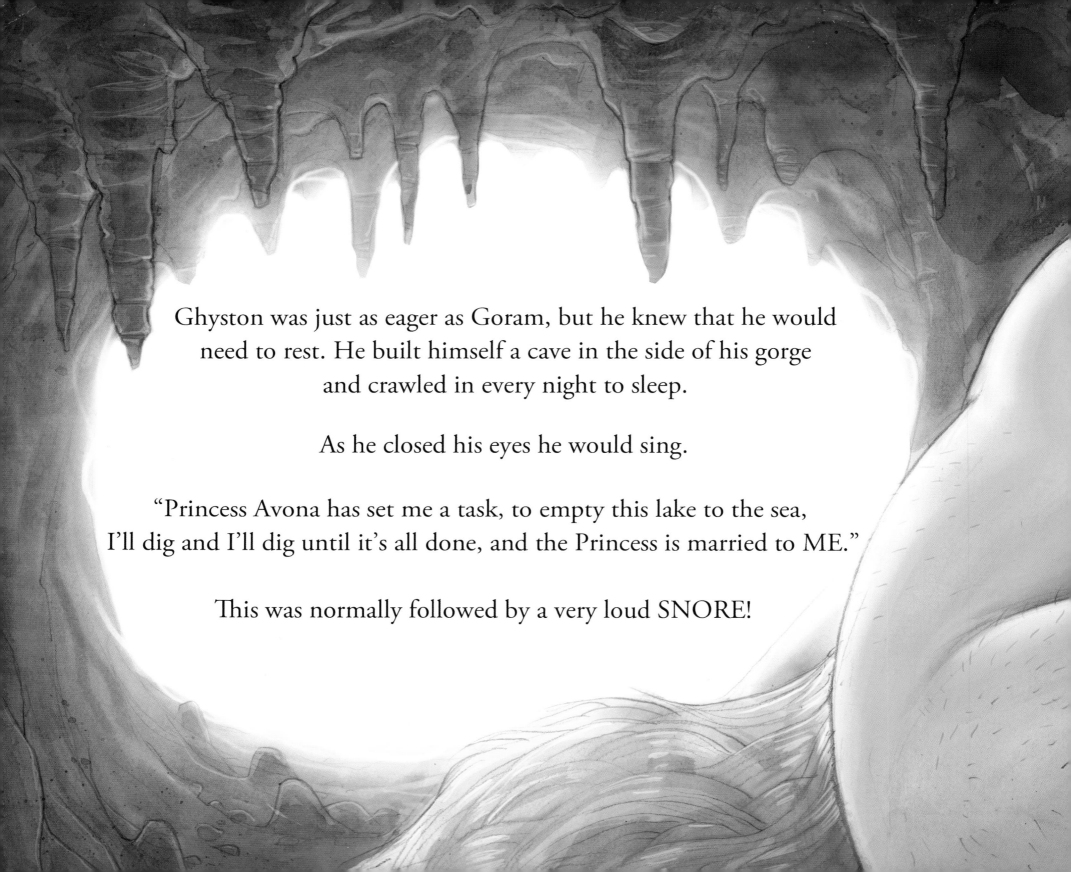

Ghyston was just as eager as Goram, but he knew that he would
need to rest. He built himself a cave in the side of his gorge
and crawled in every night to sleep.

As he closed his eyes he would sing.

"Princess Avona has set me a task, to empty this lake to the sea,
I'll dig and I'll dig until it's all done, and the Princess is married to ME."

This was normally followed by a very loud SNORE!

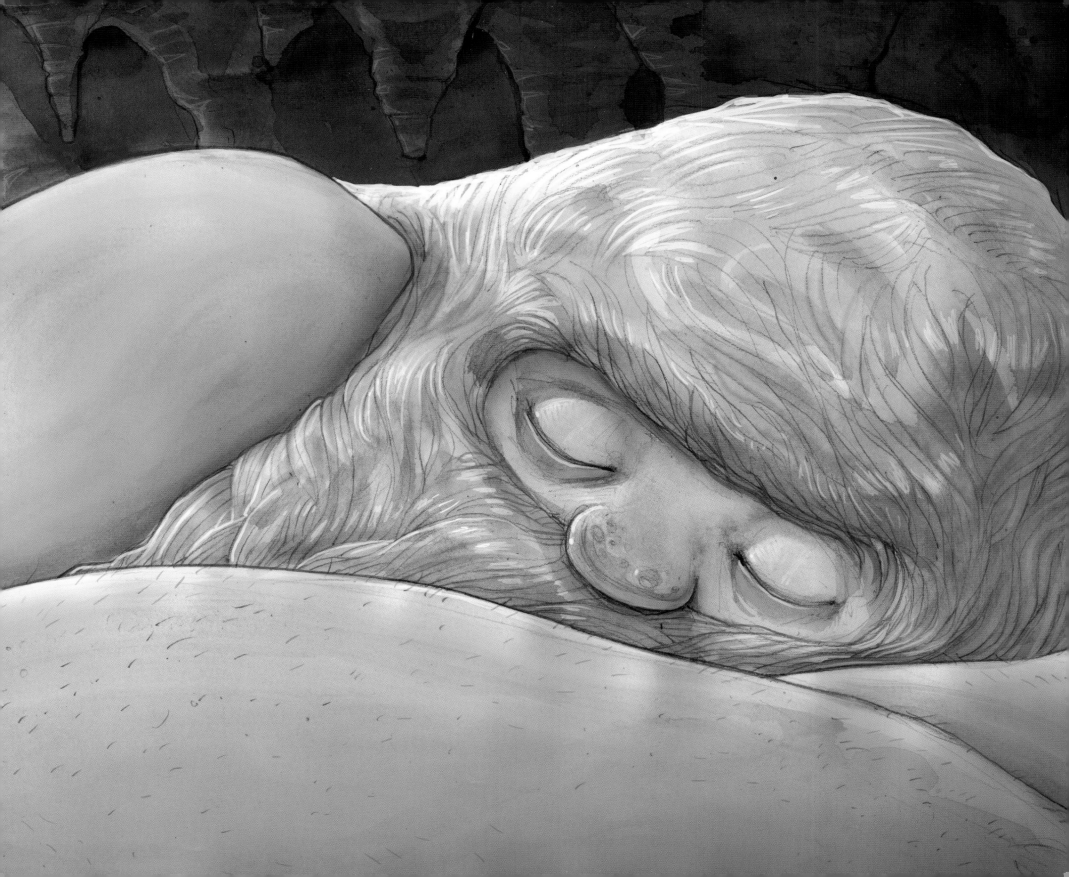

Princess Avona watched the Giants as they worked and had soon fallen in love with them both.

On and on they went for days and weeks until suddenly Goram slumped over exhausted. He built himself a chair and poured a large jug of ale. He drank the ale down in one go, burped, and immediately fell into a deep, deep sleep!

Ghyston was still a long way from the sea
but he carried on day after day – dig,
sleep, dig, sleep – until eventually, with
a final effort, he removed the last boulder.
With a huge ROAR water gushed out of the
Great Lake and down his gorge into the sea.
Within minutes the Great Lake was empty!

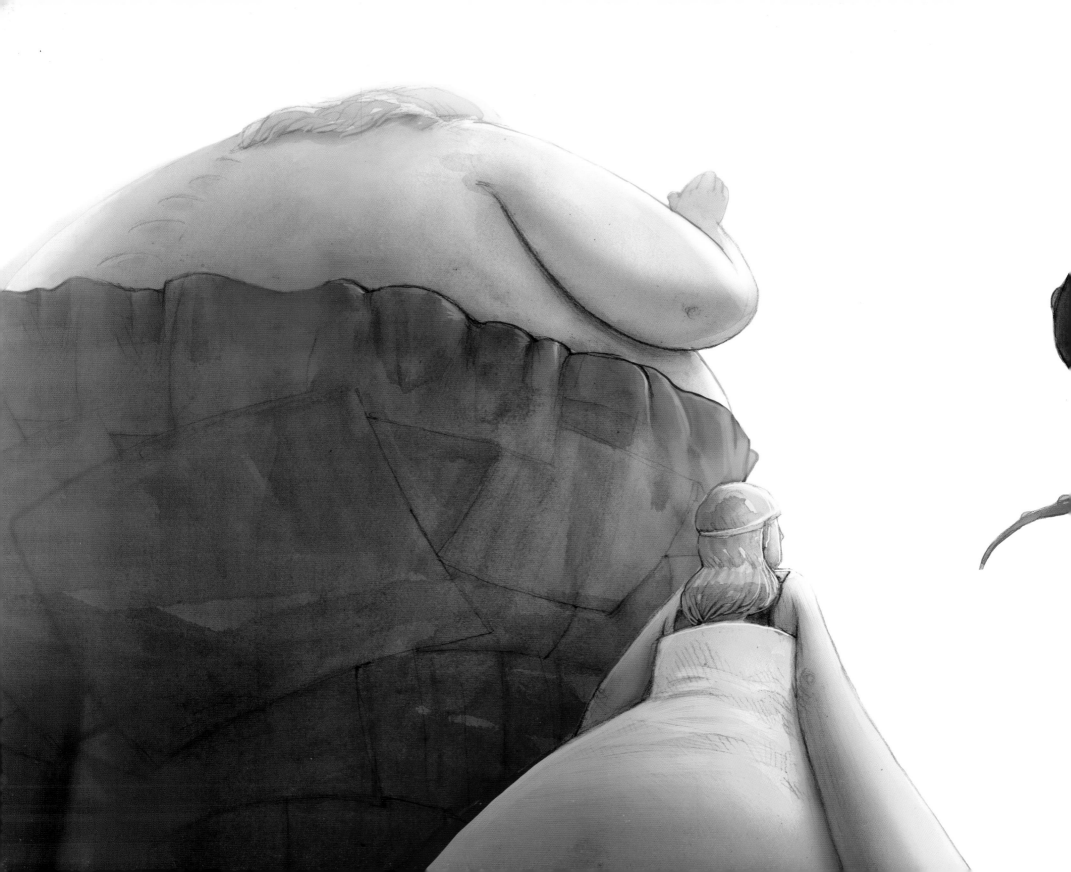

Poor Goram woke with a loud "Arumph!" and immediately realised he had lost the challenge.
He was heartbroken.

"Well done dear brother for emptying the lake and winning the Princess's heart.
I am sure I will see you again one day but now I must make a new start."

With that he jumped on his dragon Digby, waved to his brother and
Princess Avona, and flew off over the horizon.

Ghyston was very sad to say
goodbye to his brother, but overjoyed at winning
Avona's heart. They were married soon after and, as a wedding
present, he named his channel the Avon Gorge, after his Princess.

Ghyston and Princess Avona think of Goram often, and many
believe that when the Avon Gorge fills up with water, it is the
tears of the Giant and his Princess wife that swirl and
crash against the rocky walls, for they never
saw Goram again.

What happened to Goram...?

...well that is a story for another day!